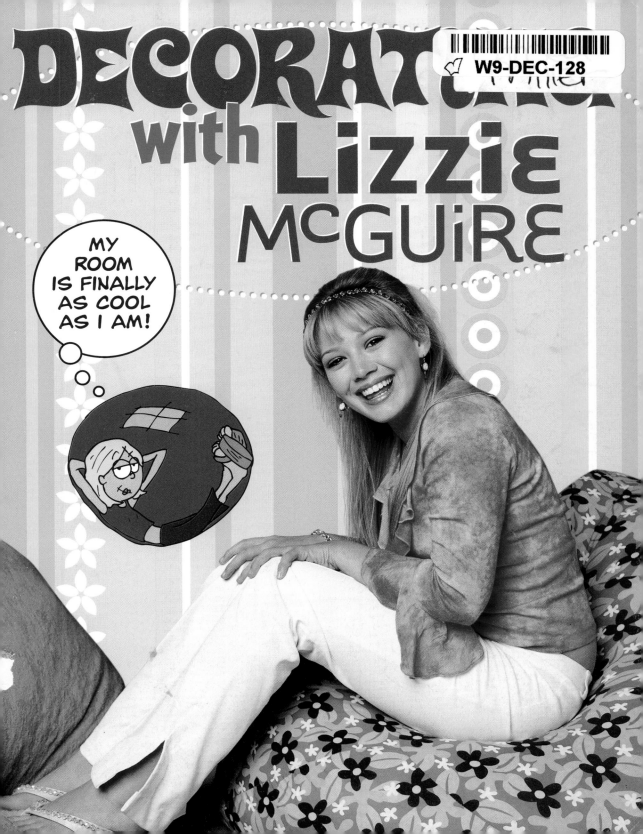

Editor: Carol Field Dahlstrom
Project Editor: Paula Marshall
Writer and Project Designer: Susan M. Banker
Designer: Angie Haupert Hoogensen
Copy Chief: Terri Fredrickson
Publishing Operations Manager: Karen Schirm
Book Production Managers: Pam Kvitne, Marjorie J. Schenkelberg,
Rick von Holdt, Mark Weaver
Contributing Copy Editor: Beth Havey
Contributing Proofreaders: Julie Cahalan, Becky Danley, Margaret Smith
Technical Illustrator: Chris Neubauer Graphics, Inc.
Project Designer: Alice Wetzel
Photostyling Assistant: Donna Chesnut
Editorial Assistants: Cheryl Eckert, Karen McFadden
Edit and Design Production Coordinator: Mary Lee Gavin

Meredith® Books
Editor in Chief: Linda Raglan Cunningham
Design Director: Matt Strelecki
Managing Editor: Gregory H. Kayko
Executive Editor, Decorating and Home Design: Denise L. Caringer

Publisher: James D. Blume
Executive Director, Marketing: Jeffrey Myers
Executive Director, New Business Development: Todd M. Davis
Executive Director, Sales: Ken Zagor
Director, Operations: George A. Susral
Director, Production: Douglas M. Johnston
Business Director: Jim Leonard

Vice President and General Manager: Douglas J. Guendel

Meredith Publishing Group
President, Publishing Group: Stephen M. Lacy
Vice President-Publishing Director: Bob Mate

Meredith Corporation
Chairman and Chief Executive Officer: William T. Kerr

In Memoriam: E.T. Meredith III (1933–2003)

Disney Publishing Worldwide, Inc.
Lisa Gerstel

Visit Lizzie every day at DisneyChannel.com

The copyright in certain projects, patterns and prints contained in
this book are owned by Meredith Corporation and are used herein under
license by Disney Enterprises, Inc.

Copyright © 2004 Disney. First Edition. Text and some
photography copyright © 2004 Meredith Corporation. First Edition.
All rights reserved. Printed in the United States of America.
Library of Congress Control Number: 2003114236
ISBN: 0-696-22012-1

We welcome your comments and suggestions. Write to us at:
Meredith Books, Crafts Editorial Department, 1716 Locust Street–LN120,
Des Moines, IA 50309-3023. Or visit us at: meredithbooks.com

DECORATING with Lizzie McGUIRE

CONTENTS

Awesome Lockers
10–15

I'm-a-Star Photo Frames
16–19

Too-Cool Chairs
20–25

All-Mine Pillows
26–29

Oh-so-Fancy Phones
30–35

B-E-A-U-tiful Boxes
36–40

Lizzie Photos
41–44

The Top Ten Ways to Use Your Photos
45

So-Cozy Throws
46–53

Wall Initials with WOW
54–57

Sensational Scrapbooks
58–63

Bright Lights
64–69

Crazy CD Cases
70–73

Sleep-Tight Pillowcases
74–79

Lizzie Stickers
back of book

GET READY TO MAKE REALLY COOL STUFF FOR YOUR PERSONAL SPACE!

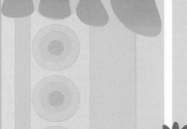

Lizzie

A NOTE FROM LIZZIE!

Decorating is where it's at!

When your friends come over for girl talk, secret sharing, and serious (not!) studying—they'll love your room filled with these sweet decorating ideas!

I'll show you how to make some totally awesome stuff—like wild chairs your friends will love and groovy phones so excellent for chitchatting.

Plus I'll help keep you oh-so-organized with creative containers for CDs, jewelry, photos, and even your school supplies. (Let me tell you girls... these locker ideas rock!)

You'll have a blast painting, decoupaging, gluing, sewing—you name it. By the time you're done, you'll know a bunch of new techniques and you'll have tons of crafts— from throws to picture frames—to show for it!

Come on, girlfriends, let's get busy!

> CRAFTING IS REALLY FUN, BUT SHOWING IT OFF IN YOUR ROOM—THAT'S PRICELESS!

WHAT KIND OF A GIRL DO YOU FEEL LIKE TODAY?

Being a girl is sooo cool! Some days you feel one way and sometimes another! Take this quiz and see.

Lizzie QUIZ

#1—My favorite food is:

A. Tofu hot dogs.

B. Mac and cheese.

C. Pizza in the shape of a flower.

Write down your points! A=1, B=3, C=2.

> BOY MEETS GIRL, GIRL FALLS FOR BOY...I LOVE HAPPY ENDINGS!

#2—When I read:

A. I wear sunglasses, 'cause I'm really sleeping with a book in my hand.

B. I pick a romantic, gushy novel.

C. You know I have serious homework!

Write down your points! A=1, B=3, C=2.

#3—My favorite day is:

A. Every day, because life rocks!

B. Saturday, because it is the weekend and I'm shopping!

C. Monday, because I have my homework done and I'm ready for school.

Write down your points! A=1, B=2, C=3.

6

#4—When I shop:

A I make a list of what I need and want.

B I buy whatever the mannequin is sportin'!

C I don't shop—I make all of my clothes out of duct tape.

Write down your points! A=3, B=2, C=1.

#5—My pet is:

A A python.

B A Persian cat with a pink ribbon around its neck.

C A dog!

Write down your points! A=1, B=2, C=3.

I'VE ALWAYS DREAMED OF HAVING A SILVER MANX CAT!

#6—I talk on the phone:

A To make sure I get the scoop on the all the news!

B To keep in touch with my ultracool girlfriends.

C And go a little crazy when a cute guy calls.

Write down your points! A=2, B=3, C=1.

#7—My closet is:

A So together—my sweaters folded nicely and my shoes in boxes.

B Painted purple with pink polka dots.

C Filled with cool musical instruments so I keep my clothes under the bed!

Write down your points! A=3, B=2, C=1.

Lizzie QUIZ

#8—My bedspread is:

A. Under a pile of clothes... somewhere!

B. So pretty I want to make it into a skirt and matching purse.

C. Colorful, like a rainbow.

Write down your points! A=1, B=2, C=3.

IF PINK IS MY HUE, THEN WHY DOESN'T IT WORK AS A HAIR COLOR?

#9—A bad hair day is:

A. When my highlights turn blue.

B. When I have to comb it.

C. When I spend 45 minutes stylin' it and I get caught in the sprinkler.

Write down your points! A=2, B=3, C=1.

#10—I love summer because:

A. I don't need a jacket every time I leave the house.

B. I can work on my tan and wear cool swimsuits.

C. Every day I have a happy-go-lucky weekend attitude!

Write down your points! A=3, B=2, C=1.

#11—School rocks because:

A. I learn new things every day.

B. I love to eat the cafeteria food, like California corn dogs and pineapple pizza!

C. I get to hang out with old friends and make new ones.

SERIOUSLY COOL!

Write down your points! A=3, B=1, C=2.

#12—My favorite color is:

A Bright pink (my friends say it's a hip color on me!)
B Red (the color of hair I've always wanted!)
C Purple (just because!)

Write down your points! A=2, B=3, C=1.

Now total your quiz points. If they total 29-36, you are ORGANIZED and always on top of things!

ORGANIZED Maybe you prefer things to be symmetrical. When you arrange things on your dresser, you balance them with one thing in the middle and equal things on both sides. And you really have to be able to find your favorite hoop earrings when you're in a hurry, so you keep your jewelry organized in your dresser drawer.

If your points total 20-28, you are arty and always stylin'!

STYLIN' You probably like to paint or decorate everything you own and you doodle on everything. Remember those new jeans? You just had to add some glitter paint on the back pockets! And the pictures on your walls are always asymmetrical–you have to have them just a little off balance!

If your points total 12-19, you are totally out of control!

OUT OF CONTROL You always seem to see the wildest side of things–you love to have your hair match your pink flip-flops and your room has your favorite photos stuck to the ceiling with chewing gum.

Each time you take the quiz, you may get a different score. But hey, it's okay that you feel like a different person each day, 'cause that's just one of the cool things about being a girl! Now, find a project that matches your mood of the moment and have fun crafting and decorating!

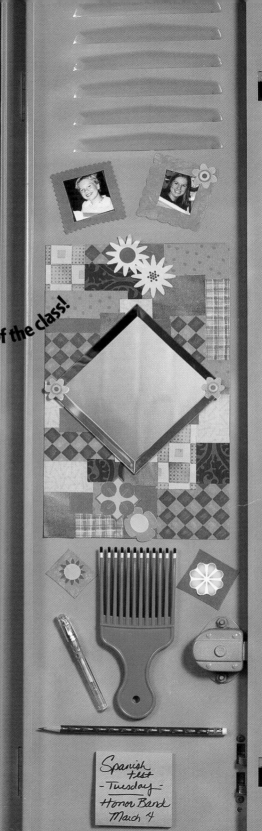

Apply your decorating know-how to your supercool school locker and be the talk of the class!

STYLIN'

Spanish
test
-Tuesday-
Honor Band
March 4

Awesome Lockers

OUT OF CONTROL

ORGANIZED

Turn the page for instructions to make these cool lockers.

TOTALLY ME!

What girl necessities do you absolutely have to keep in your locker? A mirror? A toothbrush? A mall emergency telephone list? Here are great ways to keep 'em handy!

WHAT YOU NEED

For the orange locker

Square lightweight mirror

Adhesive-back magnetic sheet

Assorted decorative scrapbook papers

Scissors or paper cutter; strong adhesive, such as E6000

Lizzie stickers from the back of the book

Photocopier, optional; decorative-edge scissors

Cutting mat or surface; crafts knife

Small button magnets; comb; pencil; notepad

HERE'S HOW

1 Measure your locker and choose a mirror to fit. Cut the magnetic sheet at least 1 inch larger on all sides than the mirror, using a paper cutter or scissors.

2 Remove the protective paper from the magnetic sheet and lay it sticky side up on a work surface. Cut small squares of decorative papers and arrange them on the sticky side, making a quilt-like pattern until the entire surface is filled. Trim off the edges if needed.

3 Spread strong adhesive on the back of the mirror. Place it on the magnet. Let dry.

4 Apply stickers to magnet. If you wish, take stickers to a photocopy store and have them enlarged; trim them out and glue onto magnet.

5 To make a picture frame, apply decorative papers to the sticky side of magnetic sheet as shown in Photo A, opposite. Cut out frame with decorative-edge scissors as shown in Photo B. Place the frame on a cutting surface and ask an adult to use a crafts knife to cut out the center as shown in Photo C. Place a photo behind the frame.

6 Add magnets to the backs of items you wish to hang in your locker. Glue small magnets to a comb. Cut long narrow strips of magnetic sheet to stick to a pencil and pen. Cut a square of magnetic sheet to stick on the back of a notepad.

I WONDER IF THE PRINCIPAL WOULD MIND IF I PAINT MY LOCKER LIME GREEN.

A B

C

WHAT YOU NEED

For the red locker

Square lightweight mirror

Adhesive-back magnetic sheet; scrapbook papers

Strong adhesive, such as E6000

Scissors or paper cutter

Lizzie stickers from back of book

Lunch ticket; white rickrack; thick white crafts glue

Decorative-edge scissors

Alphabet stickers; crafts knife; ruler

Small button magnets; comb; pencil; notepad

CONTINUED ON PAGE 14

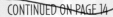

Awesome Lockers
continued

HERE'S HOW

1 Measure your locker and choose a mirror to fit. Use scissors or a paper cutter to cut the magnet piece at least 1 inch larger than the mirror.

2 Remove the protective sheet from the sticky side of the magnet and press it on a piece of scrapbook paper.

3 Spread an even coat of strong adhesive on the back of the mirror and place it in the center of magnet-backed scrapbook paper. Let dry.

4 Cut white rickrack and glue on the edge of the scrapbook paper. Add flower stickers in the corners, adding crafts glue if needed.

5 To make the picture frame and lunch ticket magnets, apply the paper to the sticky side of magnetic sheet before trimming to size. (See photos A–C on page 13 for help.) If you wish, use decorative-edge scissors to trim the outside . Use alphabet stickers to label.

DO YOU THINK 674 PHOTOS OF MY BOYFRIEND ARE TOO MANY TO PUT IN MY LOCKER?

6 To cut out the inside of the picture frame, use a ruler and a crafts knife. (Ask an adult for help!)

7 Glue magnets to the backs of other items. Glue small button magnets to the comb. Cut a long narrow strip from the magnetic sheet to hold a pencil. Cut a square to hold a notepad.

WHAT YOU NEED
For the purple locker

Assorted decorative papers

Pencil; markers in hot pink and black

Adhesive-back magnetic sheet

Scissors

Stiff adhesive-back black felt

Small gems; 2 small round mirrors

2 large gems

Strong adhesive, such as E6000

Thick white crafts glue

Alphabet stickers

Lizzie stickers from the back of the book

Metallic pom-poms; small button magnets

Comb; pen; notepad

A   B

HERE'S HOW

1 Draw a large oval on the decorative paper. Draw a nose and mouth on the oval, using the photo, page 11, for ideas. Use a marker to color hot pink lips. Outline the lips with black.

2 Remove the protective paper from the magnetic sheet. Apply the colored paper to the sticky side of magnet. Trim with scissors.

3 Lay the small round mirrors on the non-sticky side of the adhesive-back felt and trace a circle around each. Draw eyelashes around the circle as shown in Photo A, above. Cut out. Using strong adhesive, glue a round mirror in the center of each black felt cutout.

4 Use a generous amount of white crafts glue to glue a large gem at the edge of each mirror eye as shown in Photo B. Apply small gems to the tips of the eyelashes. Let dry overnight.

5 Remove the paper backing from felt and press the eyes on the oval face.

6 Use alphabet stickers to spell a word or phrase on decorative paper. Place the paper on the sticky side of the magnetic sheet and trim out whatever shape you want with scissors. Outline the letters with a black marker if you wish.

7 Apply stickers to sticky side of magnetic sheet and trim out with scissors. Add magnets to items you wish to hang in your locker. Glue small button magnets to a comb. Cut a long narrow strip of sheet magnet to stick to a favorite pen. Cut a piece of magnet to stick on back of notepad. Glue pom-poms to button magnets to make decorative magnets.

STYLIN'

These frames will highlight your amazing, wonderful face, and shout out your artistic talent too.

I'm-a-Star Photo Frames

ORGANIZED

OUT OF CONTROL

Turn the page for instructions to make these cool frames.

TOTALLY ME!

Today if you're feeling totally out of control, wear two different earrings—you might get some strange looks, but you may meet some cool new friends!

Seriously Cool!

WHAT YOU NEED

For the green frame

Square frame in a color you like; scissors; cardboard
Black card stock; decorative paper; wide black marker
Photo; glue stick; decorative string
Thick white crafts glue; tape; beads with large holes

HERE'S HOW

1. Carefully remove glass and backing from the frame.

2. Cut a piece of cardboard smaller than the frame.

3. Color the edge of the cardboard black. Cut a piece of black card stock the same size as the cardboard and glue onto cardboard. Cut a slightly smaller piece of decorative paper and glue onto the black paper for a border. Cut the photo smaller than the decorative paper. Use a glue stick to glue the photo on black card stock and trim a narrow border. Glue the mounted photo on the decorative paper.

4. Cut two pieces of string, each slightly longer than the frame height. For each string, tie a bead on one end and thread beads onto the string, leaving spaces. Don't bead the string that wraps to the back. Knot the string ends after the last beads are in place.

5. Use crafts glue to mount photo to strings. Tape the back to hold firmly.

I LOVE GOLD FRAMES! I FEEL LIKE THE MONA LISA! OR IS IT MONA LIZZIE?!

WHAT YOU NEED

For the gold frame

Fancy gold frame; scissors; cardboard
Black card stock; decorative paper
Wide black marker; photo; glue stick
Beading string; beads; thick white crafts glue; tape

HERE'S HOW

1. Follow Steps 1–3 for the green frame, opposite.

2. Cut beading string long enough to hang on frame like a necklace. Tie a bead on one end and string beads onto the center of beading string to arrange above the photo. Knot the string together where the beads end. Don't bead the string that wraps to the back. Bead string tails to hang below the photo. Tie the last bead onto each string and clip off the excess. Glue mounted photo to strings; use tape on back of photo to hold firmly.

3. Use crafts glue to attach the beaded string to the back of the frame, taping to hold in place while drying.

WHAT YOU NEED

For the turquoise frame

Plain, flat, wide frame in a color you like

Cardboard; black paper; metallic sticky-back paper

Wide black marking pen

Scissors; photo

Glue stick

Pipe cleaners

Beads to fit pipe cleaners

Thick white crafts glue

Tape

HERE'S HOW

1. Carefully remove glass and backing from the frame.

2. Cut a piece of cardboard in a shape to overlap the frame edges when placed at an angle.

3. Color the edge of the cardboard black. Cut a piece of black card stock the same size as the cardboard; glue it onto cardboard. Cut a slightly smaller and different shape piece of metallic paper; stick onto the black paper. Cut the photo smaller than the metallic paper. Glue the photo on black card stock and trim an uneven narrow border. Glue the mounted photo on the metallic paper.

4. Angle the mounted photo and glue three of the corners to the frame.

5. Fold a pipe cleaner in half and thread a few beads on each end. Shape the ends in spirals and curlicues. Glue the fold of the pipe cleaner to the back of the mounted photo, taping to hold in place while drying.

I'M SO OUT OF CONTROL I'M ADDING FIVE MORE PIPE CLEANERS TO MY FRAME!

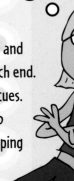

19

OUT OF CONTROL

Whether you're doing your homework or taking a break, these stylin' chairs will help you take a load off.

Too-Cool Chairs

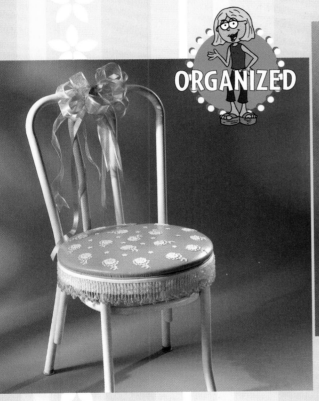

ORGANIZED

STYLIN'

Turn the page for instructions to make these cool chairs.

TOTALLY ME!

Turning trash into treasure is tons of fun and good for the environment! Get Mom to take you to thrift shops and flea markets to find chairs to decorate in your style.

WHAT YOU NEED

For the blue chair

Bentwood chair; blue acrylic paint; paintbrush

Lace appliqués or strand of lace cut apart; scissors

Matte-finish decoupage medium

Beaded trim for seat

Strong adhesive, such as E6000

4 yards of wide ribbon; 4 yards of narrow ribbon

I'M IN A BEANBAG MOOD...I WONDER WHAT I COULD DO WITH ONE OF THOSE?!

HERE'S HOW

1 Begin with a clean dry chair. Paint the seat blue using acrylic paint. Paint two or three coats as needed, letting each coat dry.

2 Arrange lace appliqués or a strand of lace and cut it apart. Decide how you want them to look. Brush the decoupage medium onto the blue seat. Lay the appliqués in wet decoupage medium. Brush over appliqués again. Let dry and brush two more coats of decoupage medium onto the surface, working it well into lace pieces.

3 Cut beaded trim to fit around chair seat. Spread a generous amount of adhesive onto back side of trim using a plastic knife or other disposable utensil. Apply to chair seat edge.

4 Make a large bow with really long tails from wide ribbon. Make another bow from the narrow ribbon. Tie them together on the chair back using narrow ribbon. Trim tails if needed.

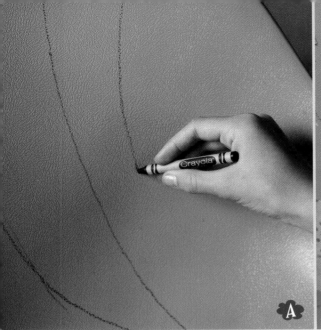

A B

WHAT YOU NEED

For the artsy chair

Molded plastic chair; marker or crayon
Assorted scraps of fabric; iron; scissors
Decoupage medium; paintbrush; 1/4-inch twill trim

HERE'S HOW

1 Draw random swirls or any pattern using a crayon or marker as shown in Photo A, above.

2 Iron the fabrics if needed (ask an adult for help). Cut the fabrics into different size squares and rectangles. Sort the light colors from the darker bright colors.

3 Brush a generous amount of decoupage medium onto a section of chair. Lay fabrics onto wet decoupage medium. Brush over the fabric as you add pieces, smoothing out wrinkles as you go, as shown in Photo B. Fill in sections with fabric pieces.

4 Trim and define the sections with black twill ribbon. Clip the trim along the edges to make curves. As in Step 3, use decoupage medium to apply them to the chair.

5 Coat the entire chair with decoupage medium. Let dry.

CONTINUED ON PAGE 24

fashion. all over it!

fashion. all over it!

WHAT YOU NEED

For the feathered chair

Wooden chair with fabric seat

Acrylic paint for seat and chair (if needed)
  and a paintbrush; matte-finish decoupage medium

Small and large feathers for seat, back, and top back

Feather boa for trim around seat

Fabric braid trim for feather quills

Strong adhesive, such as E6000

HERE'S HOW

1 Use your chair as it is or paint it as this one was. Paint the seat with two coats of white or any color of acrylic paint. Let dry.

2 Arrange small feathers on the seat. Brush a section at a time with a generous amount of matte-finish decoupage medium. Carefully lay feathers into the decoupage medium. Brush decoupage medium over feathers. Be careful to brush the feathers once in the direction you want them to lie. Don't swirl them around or brush back and forth. Let the decoupage medium dry. Apply another coat of decoupage medium and let dry.

3 Use adhesive to glue small feathers to the back side of chair as shown in Photo A, below. Trim feather boa to fit around seat of chair and glue it by dabbing a generous spot of adhesive every 2 or 3 inches.

4 Cut braided trim to fit chair back. Glue trim to cover the glue and quills neatly.

5 Glue two large feathers onto the back side of the chair. Cover the area as in Step 4 with a piece of braided trim.

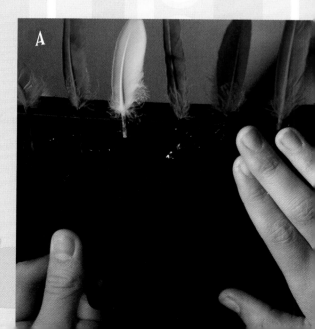

A

Use the techniques you learned for the chairs to decorate:

❀ Desks (at home, not school!)

❀ Bed headboards and footboards

❀ Filing cabinets (yours, not Dad's!)

❀ Bookcases and shelves

❀ Dressers

❀ Storage containers (such as wood boxes, baskets, and plastic tubs)

❀ Mirrors

❀ Stools

❀ Hope chests (where you keep all your special treasures!)

❀ Benches

❀ Picture frames

Before you start Lizzie-izing your room, be sure to get the OK from Mom or Dad. They might have some suggestions for you (or they may want to join in the fun!).

MY ROOM IS SOOO COOL, I'M NEVER LEAVING IT! (EXCEPT TO EAT, SHOP, CHAT...)

STYLIN'

Zip up your bedroom space with adorable pillows that burst with personality plus!

All-Mine Pillows

ORGANIZED

LM

OUT OF CONTROL

Turn the page for instructions to make these cool pillows.

TOTALLY ME!

Look how totally different these pillow styles are! The next time you choose bedding, try something in a solid color. Then change your pillows to fit your mood!

WHAT YOU NEED

For the checked pillow

Purchased black-and-white checked pillow

Felt in black, red, and white

Iron and ironing surface (if needed); pinking shears

Scissors; 4 buttons; needle and thread

Purchased embroidered or felt letters; fabric glue

HERE'S HOW

1 Use pinking shears or scissors to cut three squares from the three colors of felt. Cut the squares three different sizes, the largest black and the red slightly larger than the smallest white piece. Ask an adult to help you press the felt pieces if needed.

2 Center the white felt square on the red square. Sew a button in each corner of the white square, sewing through both layers.

3 Use fabric glue to attach the felt initials in the square center.

4 Spread an even amount of fabric glue onto the back side of the black piece of felt and glue it in place on the

pillow center. Spread an even amount of glue onto the back side of the red square and glue it on the black square.

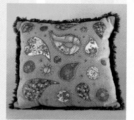

WHAT YOU NEED

For the denim paisley pillow

Purchased denim pillow; tracing paper; pencil

Scissors; assorted fabrics

Iron and ironing surface (if needed)

Fabric glue; gold glitter tube paint

I'M GOING TO GLUE SILK BUTTERFLIES AND FLOWERS TO MY NEXT PILLOW!

HERE'S HOW

1 Trace the paisley shapes, below, on tracing paper, cut out, and lay on fabric.

2 Using pencil, trace paisley shapes and small circles on assorted fabrics. Cut out and press fabric shapes if needed.

3 Arrange the shapes on the denim pillow as you like. Remove one fabric piece at a time and use your finger to spread an even layer of glue onto the back side of fabric, covering all of the surface and the edges. Place onto pillow

and smooth out. If fabric piece doesn't stick, add more glue. If glue oozes out the edges, you are using too much.

4 Outline the shapes and circles and draw small dots using tube paint. Let dry.

WHAT YOU NEED

For the frog pillow

Purchased velveteen pillow; stuffed frog
Needle; thread; white fur trim; tracing paper; pencil
Felt in hot pink and purple; scissors; fabric glue

HERE'S HOW

1 Position the stuffed frog on the pillow. Use a needle and thread to sew his legs in place.

2 Cut a rectangle from purple felt to fit under the frog. Place a piece of white fur trim under the frog and around the pillow.

3 Trace lip pattern, below, onto tracing paper, and cut out. Trace onto pink felt 10 times. Cut out and glue onto pillow. Let dry.

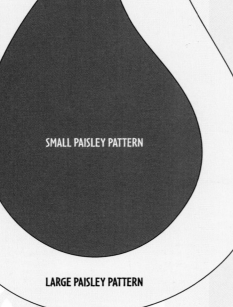

SMALL PAISLEY PATTERN

LARGE PAISLEY PATTERN

LIPS PATTERN

Chitchatting will be even more fun on a supercool painted phone!

Oh-so-Fancy Phones

ORGANIZED

OUT OF CONTROL

Turn the page for instructions to make these cool phones.

TOTALLY ME!

Phones come in a zillion shapes and colors. Pick the style you like best, and if the color isn't just right—paint it! (Just be careful not to plug up any essential parts!)

WHAT YOU NEED

For the black phone

Black purse-style phone

Acrylic enamel paints in red, orange, orange-yellow, yellow, green, turquoise, and purple

Paper plate; pencils with round-tip erasers

HERE'S HOW

1. Wipe the phone with a damp cloth and let it dry. Avoid touching the areas to be painted.

2. Put a very small amount of each paint color in a lid and place on a paper plate.

3. Starting with red, dab a pencil eraser end in the paint as shown in Photo A, below left. Dot the paint onto the phone, using a different pencil for each color. Make a circle of dots ¼ inch apart around the phone in the order shown in the photo on page 30. (This phone has a ridge to use as a guide.) Let the paint dry.

WHAT YOU NEED

For the floral phone

White phone

Acrylic enamel paints in pink, purple, lime green, and black

Paper plate; paintbrushes

HERE'S HOW

1. Wipe the phone with a damp cloth and let it dry. Avoid touching the areas to be painted.

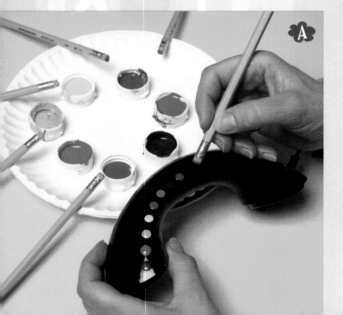

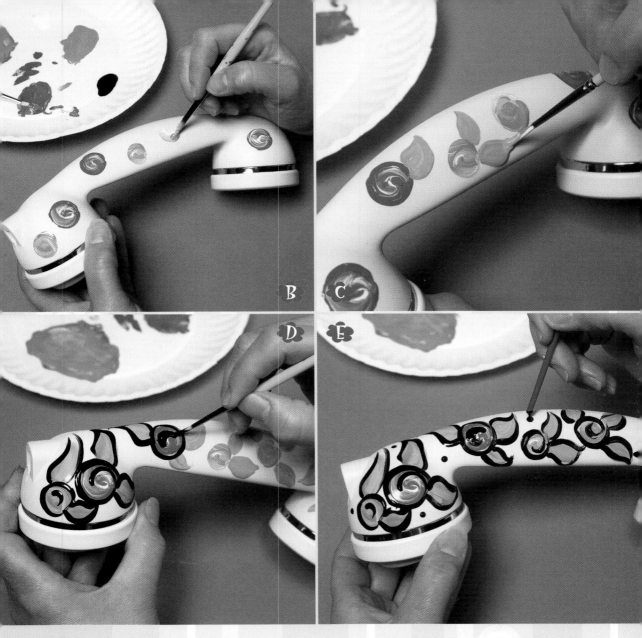

B

C

D

E

2 Put a small amount of each paint color on the plate. Paint pink and purple flower dots ranging from dime to nickel size on the receiver as shown in Photo B, above. Paint the dial center pink.

3 Paint simple green leaves next to and between the flowers as shown in Photo C. Let the paint dry.

4 Paint black stripes on the receiver and at the base of the phone. Loosely outline and detail the leaves and flowers as shown in Photo D. To make dots, dip the paintbrush handle in paint and dot between flowers as shown in Photo E. Let dry.

CONTINUED ON PAGE 34

Oh-so-Fancy Phones

WHAT YOU NEED

For the jeweled phone

Black phone

Acrylic enamel paints in silver, metallic turquoise, metallic pink, metallic purple, and black

Paintbrush; paper plate

1/8-inch-wide silver hologram sticker strips; large purple flat sequins

Assorted plastic gems in pink, purple, turquoise, and clear

Gem glue

HERE'S HOW

1 Wipe the phone with a damp cloth and let it dry. Avoid touching the areas to be painted.

IF I PAINT MY PHONE BRIGHT PINK, WOULD MY BROTHER KEEP HIS HANDS OFF?

2 Put a very small amount of each paint color on a paper plate.

3 Starting with one color, make random brush strokes on the base of the phone as shown in Photo A, below. Change colors and continue the process until all colors are used and the phone base is covered with paint. Let the paint dry.

4 For the trims, cut short pieces of the sticker strips. Using glue to adhere the sequins and gems, trim the phone face, dial center, and receiver top. Let the glue dry.

A

Use the techniques you learned for the phones to paint:

* ❉ Canvas tennis shoes (use fabric paint or mix textile medium with acrylic paint)
* ❉ Clothes hamper
* ❉ Your bedroom walls (don't forget the drop cloth!)
* ❉ A mirror frame
* ❉ A personalized sign for your room (Girls Only, My Space, or your name)
* ❉ A CD holder
* ❉ All of your furniture in all your favorite colors
* ❉ A chair
* ❉ Tiny stuff, such as sunglass cases, jewelry boxes, and makeup cases
* ❉ An old purse or belt

When painting, read the paint labels to be sure you're using the right kind of paint for the surface you're painting. Otherwise the paint may flake or scrape off—and that would be a bummer!

I DID IT! I DID IT! I PAINTED MY SHOES—ON PURPOSE! (AND THEY'RE SO SWEEEET!)

ORGANIZED

Your friends will be like soooo jealous of these extra-neat trinket boxes!

B-E-A-U-tiful Boxes

OUT OF CONTROL

STYLIN'

Turn the page for instructions to make these cool boxes.

TOTALLY ME!

Girls can never have too many containers to keep all their treasures! These tiny boxes are just right for storing jewelry, makeup, and all the other essentials!

B-E-A-U-tiful Boxes
continued

WHAT YOU NEED
For the black box

Unfinished or black wood box with drawers
  (available at discount and crafts stores)
Black acrylic enamel paint and paintbrush, optional
Photocopies of your own photos
Scissors; foam alphabet and floral stickers
Decoupage medium

HERE'S HOW

1. If you have an unfinished wood box, paint it with acrylic enamel paint and let dry.

2. Cut out photocopies of your photos to fit the top and front of the box, leaving room for your name at the top of each drawer. If the drawers have knobs, cut a slit in the center of the photo (see Photo A, opposite) and cut a small circle to allow for the knob.

3. Coat the back of each photo with decoupage medium and press into place on the box. Coat the top of the photos with decoupage medium. Let dry.

4. On each drawer, spell out your name. Press floral stickers on the box sides.

WHAT YOU NEED
For the white box

Unfinished or white wood box with drawers
  (available at discount and crafts stores)
White acrylic enamel paint and paintbrush, optional
Pencil; scissors
Bright solid colors of origami paper
Decoupage medium
Photocopies of your own photos
Lizzie stickers from the
  back of the book
4 foam floral stickers

I WONDER IF I CAN FIND A BOX BIG ENOUGH TO HOLD MY HAIR ACCESSORIES?

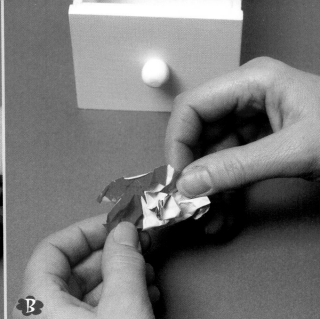

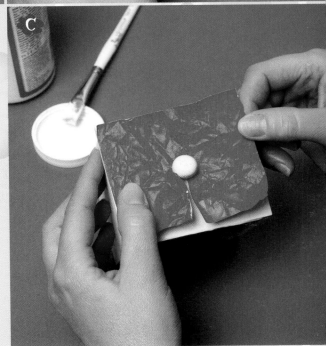

HERE'S HOW

1. If you have an unfinished wood box, paint it with acrylic enamel paint and let dry.

2. Remove the drawers from the box. Use the drawers as patterns to cut origami papers to apply to the drawer fronts. Trace around drawer fronts on origami papers and cut out. If the drawers have knobs, mark and cut a slit up the center of each paper piece as shown in Photo A, above; cut a small circle to allow for the knob. Crinkle the paper with your hands as shown in Photo B; smooth out. Use decoupage medium to glue papers to drawer fronts, as shown in Photo C.

3. Cut varying widths and colors from origami paper to cover the box top, leaving a 1/4-inch border. Use decoupage medium to glue paper pieces to box top. Cut out your photo photocopies and decoupage over the origami strips.

Add Lizzie stickers. Coat the box top and drawer fronts with decoupage medium and let dry. Stick a foam flower in each corner of the box top.

CONTINUED ON PAGE 40

39

B-E-A-U-tiful Boxes
continued

WHAT YOU NEED

For the pink box

Unfinished or hot pink wood box

Hot pink acrylic enamel paint; paintbrush, optional

Photocopies of your own photos

Scissors; circle cutter

Scrapbook papers; foam stickers

Decoupage medium

Lizzie stickers from the back of the book

HERE'S HOW

1. If you have an unfinished wood box, paint it with acrylic enamel paint and let dry.

2. Cut out photocopies of your photos using scissors and a circle cutter.

3. Cut strips and circles from scrapbook papers. Arrange the photos and paper shapes on the box, avoiding the knobs if necessary. Coat the back sides with decoupage medium and press into place on the box. When all paper shapes are glued to the box, coat the entire box with decoupage medium. Let dry.

4. Press foam and Lizzie stickers on the box.

40

THE TOP TEN WAYS TO USE YOUR PHOTOS

10 Decoupage photos on the frame of a wall mirror for a way-cool room mirror!

9 Laminate strips of photos to make bookmarks for all your awesome friends!

8 Use fabric transfer sheets (available where computer papers are sold) to put your photo face on your pillowcase!

7 Use a glue stick to glue photos to posterboard to hang in your room!

6 Make collages of family photos and laminate them to use as place mats!

5 Make lots of photocopies and glue to a wallpaper border for your room!

4 Use fabric transfer sheets to put your favorite photo on a T-shirt!

3 Decoupage your photos all over a pair of canvas shoes!

2 Cover a plain notebook cover with a collage of your photos!

1 Attach photos to adhesive-backed magnets to put all over the fridge and your locker!

OUT OF CONTROL

Cuddle under one of these comfy fleece throws

and chat, chat, chat or nap, nap, nap!

So-Cozy Throws

STYLIN'

ORGANIZED

Turn the page for instructions to make these cozy throws.

TOTALLY ME!

With a couple of hand-stitched blankets and a reversible bedspread, I can change the look of my room—season after beautiful season!

WHAT YOU NEED

For the heart-trim throw

Tracing paper

Pencil

Scissors

Felt in bright pink and dark red

Embroidery floss in bright and dark pink

Needle

Blue fleece throw

Four ½-inch buttons
  and one 1-inch
  button in
  bright pink

Fabric glue

I THINK I'LL UPDATE MY JEAN JACKET WITH SOME FELT HEARTS AND BUTTONS.

HERE'S HOW

1 Trace the heart pattern on page 52 and the flower center pattern on page 53. Cut out and trace around the heart pattern on bright pink felt five times and dark red felt four times. Trace the flower center pattern on dark red. Cut out the shapes.

2 Use contrasting embroidery floss to sew long running stitches, see diagram below, along the center of each heart.

3 Glue the bright pink hearts in the center of one end of the throw to form a flower. Glue the flower center in the center of it and two dark red hearts on each side of the heart flower. Sew the large button in the center of the felt circle and a small button near the point of each dark red heart.

RUNNING STITCH

WHAT YOU NEED

For the circle-trim throw

Tracing paper; pencil

Scissors

Felt in turquoise and purple

Embroidery floss in purple, turquoise, and orange

Needle

Assorted buttons in lime green, purple, orange,
   and turquoise

Yellow fleece throw

Fabric glue

HERE'S HOW

1 Trace the large circle pattern on page 53.
   Cut out and trace around the pattern four
times on turquoise felt and three times on purple.
Cut out the felt circles.

2 Use contrasting embroidery floss to sew
   off-centered turquoise spokes (like a wheel)
on purple circles. Stitch purple running stitches
around the edge of the turquoise felt circles as
shown in Photo A, above; stitch an X off-center in
each circle. Stitch orange buttons to each felt circle.

3 On one end of the
   throw, evenly
arrange and glue the
circles 2 inches from the
edge. Sew the remaining
buttons around the
felt circles.

Ⓐ

THIS SEWING STUFF IS SOOOO EASY, I'M GOING TO TEACH ALL MY FRIENDS!

So-Cozy Throws
continued

WHAT YOU NEED

For the flower-trim throw

Tracing paper

Pencil

Scissors

Felt in bright colors, white, and black

Fabric glue

Small blue and assorted color buttons

Embroidery floss in white and blue

Needle

Dark red fleece throw

HERE'S HOW

1 Trace the flower, leaf, and butterfly patterns on pages 52–53. Cut out and trace around the patterns on felt as many times as desired. Cut out the felt shapes.

2 Glue felt flower centers to felt flowers; sew one or three buttons to the flower center using Photos A and B, opposite, for help. Use white embroidery floss to sew long stitches for veins on each flower and leaf petal as shown in Photo C.

3 On one end of the throw, arrange and glue the felt shapes and layer and glue the butterfly body on the wings.

4 Sew the small blue buttons randomly around the felt shapes using blue embroidery floss.

Seriously Cool!

A

B

C

I'M GOING TO SEW BRIGHT BUTTONS ON THE HEM OF MY TANK TOP!

Throw Patterns

HEART PATTERN

BUTTERFLY
BODY
PATTERN

Seriously cool

BUTTERFLY WING PATTERN

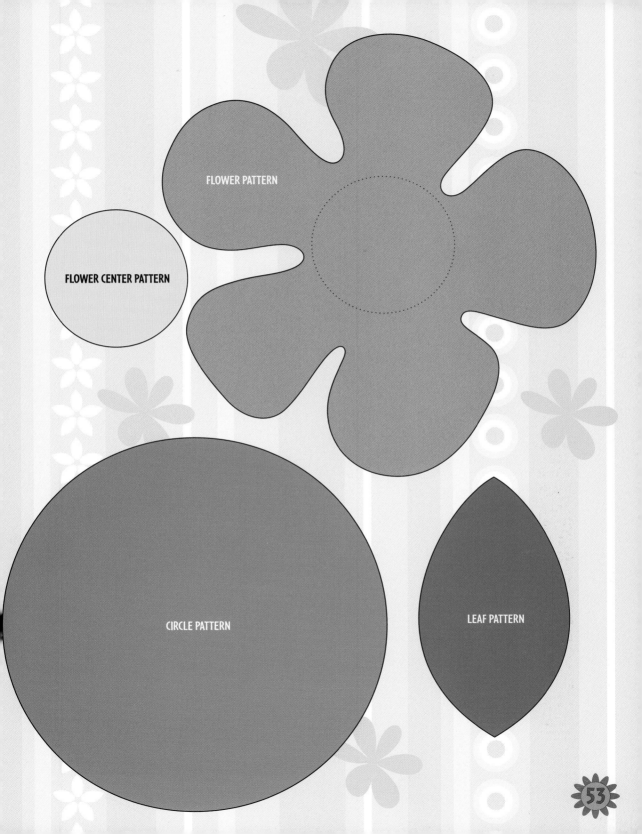

FLOWER PATTERN

FLOWER CENTER PATTERN

CIRCLE PATTERN

LEAF PATTERN

53

Choose a favorite theme to dress up your initial and make it say YOU!

ORGANIZED

Wall Initials with WOW

OUT OF CONTROL

STYLIN'

Turn the page for instructions
to make these cool initials.

Initials are hot! Make yours a
reflection of the girl you are!
Maybe you could glue on makeup
containers or musical notes.

WHAT YOU NEED

For the L (shoe theme)

Distressed wood or resin initial for your name (available in home decor, discount, and crafts stores)

Gold spray paint; metallic shoe stickers

Acrylic gems; gem glue

HERE'S HOW

1. In a well-ventilated work area, ask an adult to help you spray-paint the initial gold. Let the paint dry.

2. Arrange the stickers on the initial, gluing a gem between each sticker.

WHAT YOU NEED

For the M (sea theme)

Wood or resin initial for your name (available in home decor, discount, and crafts stores)

Silver spray paint; flat marbles in blues and clear

Shells; sea-theme die cut (available in scrapbooking stores); low-temp glue gun; glue sticks

HERE'S HOW

1. In a well-ventilated work area, ask an adult to help you spray-paint the initial silver. Let the paint dry.

2. Arrange the decorative items on the initial, covering the bottom portion with marbles. Glue the items in place.

WHAT YOU NEED

For the R (nature theme)

Wood or resin initial for your name (available in
  home decor, discount, and crafts stores)

Spray paint in periwinkle blue and white

Rocks, nest, stick, artificial eggs, silk butterflies and
  bugs, and nature items

Low-temp glue gun and glue sticks

Black permanent marking pen

HERE'S HOW

1 In a well-ventilated work area, ask an adult to
help you spray-paint the initial blue. Let the
paint dry and apply a second coat if needed. Let
dry. Using quick spurts, spray the letter with white
to add flecks over the blue. Let dry.

2 Arrange the decorative items on the initial
until you like how it looks. Glue the items in
place. Use a black marking pen to draw dotted lines
for butterfly flight patterns.

INSTEAD OF A HEADBOARD, I'M GOING TO SPELL "DREAM" ABOVE MY BED!

ORGANIZED

Keep all your prized photos and clippings in an artistically covered album.

Sensational Scrapbooks

OUT OF CONTROL

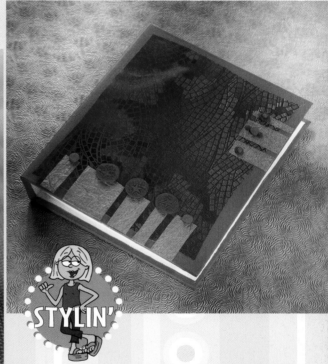

STYLIN'

Turn the page for instructions to make these cool scrapbooks.

TOTALLY ME! Share your creativity! The next time you don't know what gift to buy for someone, make them a scrapbook of the times you've shared! To carry out a theme, use stickers.

WHAT YOU NEED

For the pink cover

Scrapbook or album

Translucent, pink, and gold polymer clay, such as
  Sculpey; roller; rubber stamp; table knife

Baking dish; oven; purple highlighting medium

Stencil brush; tissue; white paper

Scissors or paper cutter; coordinating paper

Gold marker; album; spray adhesive

Strong adhesive, such as E6000

I BET I CAN MAKE SOME SWEEET BIRTHDAY CARDS WITH PAPER AND CLAY!

HERE'S HOW

1. Use equal walnut-size amounts of translucent, pink, and gold clay. Roll them into long snakes and then roll together without mixing thoroughly, as shown in Photo A, opposite.

2. Roll out the clay to about $1/8$-inch thick and large enough to fit your stamp, as shown in Photo B. Press clay firmly on stamp. If the stamp is large, pick up the stamp with the clay on it and press it with your fingers. If you don't get a good image, reroll the clay and try again. Trim off edges with a knife. Have an adult help you lay it in a baking dish and bake in an oven according to clay instructions. Let cool.

3. Brush the clay piece with highlighting medium, rubbing it into the crevices with a stencil brush as shown in Photo C. Wipe off excess medium with a tissue as shown in Photo D.

4. Cut a piece of paper a little larger than the clay piece. Tear a piece of coordinating paper to fit onto album cover. Color in the torn edge with a gold marker. Let dry.

5. Ask an adult to help you spray the back of the paper with spray adhesive, making sure you cover all of the paper. Lay down the large piece first. Lay down the smaller one next. Use strong adhesive to glue the clay piece to the front. Let dry.

CONTINUED ON PAGE 62

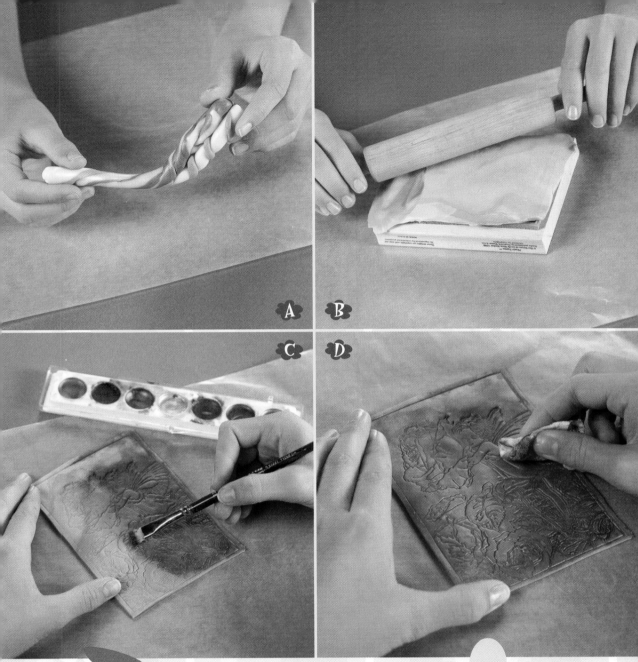

A   B

C   D

61

WHAT YOU NEED

For the red and gold cover

Scrapbook or album

2 coordinating papers, one textured solid and
  one patterned

Scissors; spray adhesive

Polymer clay, such as Sculpey, in purple and red

Rubber stamp

Baking dish

Oven

Strong adhesive, such as E6000

HERE'S HOW

1 Trim the patterned paper to fit the front of the album. The edges can be wavy and do not have to be perfectly straight. Cut smaller solid textured rectangles to be arranged however you want. Have an adult help you spray the back sides with adhesive and attach to album cover.

2 Roll out small balls of purple clay, making large grape-size pieces to fit a 1-inch square stamp. Press stamp into clay, flattening it. Roll out small balls of clay and flatten them with your fingers to create other designs. Ask an adult to bake the clay in a glass baking dish according to clay instructions. Let cool.

3 Glue on clay pieces using strong adhesive. Let dry.

WHAT YOU NEED

For the black and white cover

Scrapbook or album

Red polymer clay, such as Sculpey

Rubber letter stamps, about $\frac{1}{2}$-inch square

Baking dish; oven

Silver highlighting creme

Coordinating papers

Decorative-edge scissors

Scissors

Glue stick

Silver glitter paint

Strong adhesive, such as E6000

HERE'S HOW

1. Roll out small grape-size balls of clay for $\frac{1}{2}$-inch stamps. Make the clay balls larger if needed for your stamp. Press stamp firmly into clay until it flattens. Ask an adult to bake it in a glass baking dish according to clay instructions. Let the clay cool.

2. Put a small amount of silver highlighting medium on your fingertip and gently highlight raised areas on clay pieces.

3. Cut random size pieces of coordinating papers with decorative- and straight-edge scissors. Cover the back side of papers using glue stick and press onto album cover.

4. Use silver glitter paint to add swirls, dots, or outlines to your cover.

5. Use a small amount of strong adhesive to glue the small clay pieces to the cover. Let dry.

I LOVE TO SCRAP AND NOW I HAVE COOL SCRAPBOOKS TO FILL UP!

OUT OF CONTROL

Make your bedroom lamp reflect the real you—sweet, artsy, or totally wild!

Bright Lights

Turn the page for instructions to make these cool lamps.

Let friends sign your shade! For an organized look, use the shade edge as a guide. Write around the dots on the stylin' shade. Or write any which way for an out-of-control lamp.

Bright Lights
continued

WHAT YOU NEED
For the polka-dot lamp

Round red lamp base; solid black lampshade

Wood salad bowl (available at discount stores)

Square wood plaque to fit under bowl (available at crafts stores)

Acrylic enamel paint in blue and yellow; paintbrush

Wood glue; adhesive-back paper in yellow, black, and white; Lizzie flower stickers from the back of the book

Circle stickers in white and blue

Ruler; scissors

HERE'S HOW

1. Paint the plaque blue and the bowl yellow; let dry. Paint a second coat if needed. Let dry.

2. Apply wood glue on the bowl rim and place in the center of the square plaque. Let dry. Glue the lamp base to the bottom of the bowl.

3. Cut squares, rectangles, triangles, and strips from adhesive-back paper. Apply these and Lizzie stickers to the lamp base, using the photo for ideas. Press white circles on the shade.

WHAT YOU NEED
For the heart lamp

Simple lamp and shade

Ribbon; glue stick; scissors

Heart-shape stickers

Gold adhesive-back paper

Lizzie flower stickers from the back of the book; ruler; pencil

HERE'S HOW

1. Rub a glue stick on the back of the ribbon and glue it around

I WONDER IF I COULD PAINT PAW PRINTS ON A SHADE FOR MY KITTY-LOVIN' FRIENDS...

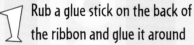

Seriously cool!

I LOVE STICKERS! SOMETIMES I PUT THEM ALL OVER MY BROTHER'S SHOES WHEN HE'S ASLEEP!

the shade top and bottom and at the lamp base, as shown in Photo A, above. Trim off the extra ribbon.

2 Place the heart-shape and Lizzie flower stickers in a straight line on lamp base. Use a ruler and pencil to draw 2-inch squares on back of gold adhesive-back paper. Cut out the squares. Stick squares in straight lines on each side of the shade. Press heart stickers on squares and flower stickers between squares as shown in Photo B. If needed, use a glue stick to help hold stickers.

CONTINUED ON PAGE 68

I LOVE THE LOOK OF GEMS! I'M GOING TO COVER THE WHOLE LAMP WITH 'EM!

Seriously cool!

WHAT YOU NEED

For the metallic lamp

Decorative lamp base; dark lampshade

Gold glitter fabric tube paint; gems

Adhesive-back metallic paper or thin vinyl
  (available in scrapbooking stores)

Scissors; floral and decorative Lizzie stickers from
  the back of the book; assorted metallic stickers

Pipe cleaners; marking pen; metallic pom-poms

HERE'S HOW

1 Squeeze dabs of glitter paint around the base of lamp and press gems into paint as shown in Photo A, opposite. Set the base aside. Let dry.

2 Cut half circles from metallic papers and arrange around lower edge of shade. Cut triangle shapes from metallic paper and arrange around the top of the shade. Fill in open spaces with assorted stickers. Outline some sticker shapes with gold metallic paint.

3 Push one end of a pipe cleaner into a pom-pom, as shown in Photo B. Wind the pipe cleaner around a marking pen. Wrap the coiled pipe cleaner on the lampshade, as shown in Photo C.

A B

C

AND MY DAD THOUGHT PIPE CLEANERS WERE FOR CLEANING PIPES!

Keep all your music organized in a colorful holder that's as clever as you are!

Crazy CD Cases

OUT OF CONTROL

ORGANIZED

Turn the page for instructions to make these cool cases.

TOTALLY ME!

If you're into music, learn all about the history! Visit a flea market and check out albums and 8-tracks. You might want to use them to decorate your room!

WHAT YOU NEED

For the mesh holder

Mesh stainless steel CD holder; narrow ribbon
Lizzie decorative stickers from the back of the book
Photocopier and glue stick, optional
Crafting foam; pencil; ruler
Scissors; thick white crafts glue

HERE'S HOW

1 Weave a narrow ribbon in and out around the top of CD holder. If the holder does not have holes in it, glue the ribbon around the rim.

2 Choose stickers from the back of the book. If you would like to use them in a smaller or larger size or would like more of one kind than is provided, you may take these to a photocopier and have them copied. Then cut them out.

3 Mark squares onto different colors of fun foam using a ruler and pencil. Cut out with scissors. Affix the Lizzie stickers on foam or use glue to attach photocopies.

4 Use white crafts glue to attach onto side of CD holder in an organized arrangement.

WHAT YOU NEED

For the plastic drawer holder

Plastic drawer CD holder
Photocopier and glue stick, optional
Paint pens
Lizzie decorative stickers from the back of the book

I HAVE SO MANY COOL CDS, I'M MAKING A HOLDER IN EACH STYLE!

HERE'S HOW

1. Choose stickers from the back of the book. If you want them larger than provided, take them to a photocopier, have them enlarged, and cut them out. Attach them with a glue stick.

2. Place stickers on CD holder. Use colored paint pens to draw zigzags, circles, short lines, and patterns, changing the colors often. Draw until all spaces are filled. Let dry.

WHAT YOU NEED

For the pink coil holder

Coil CD rack

Lizzie decorative stickers from the back of the book

Photocopier and glue stick, optional

Scissors; assorted fun foam

Pipe cleaners; strong adhesive, such as E6000

HERE'S HOW

1. Choose stickers from the back of the book. If you want them larger or smaller, take them to a photocopier and have them reproduced. Then trim them out and use a glue stick to attach them.

2. Cut shapes from different colored fun foam a little larger than the sticker you plan to use. Affix stickers to fun foam.

3. Apply a small amount of E6000 adhesive to back side of fun foam. Attach fun foam shapes to pipe cleaners and let dry.

4. Shape the pipe cleaner into a coil, zigzag, or whatever you wish.

5. Wrap one end onto the CD holder.

Get your beauty sleep on a supercool pillowcase that you stamp using neat shapes and dyes!

Sleep-Tight Pillowcases

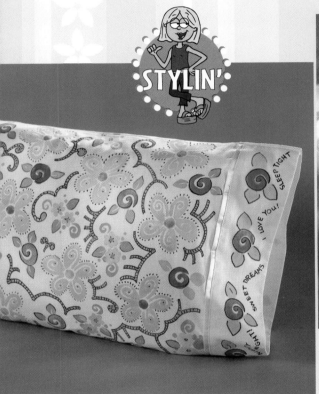

Turn the page for instructions to make these cool pillowcases.

Why stop at stamping pillowcases? Put your favorite designs on your sheets too! (And if Mom will let you, paint a few huge shapes on your wall!)

WHAT YOU NEED

For the stars pillowcase

Washed cotton pillowcase in a light color

Iron

Cardboard cut to the size of the pillowcase

Green fabric dye in a jar, such as Dye-na-flow
  by Jacquard

1-inch square star stamp

Plate; paper towel

Fabric paint markers in opaque white and green

HERE'S HOW

1. Ask an adult to iron the pillowcase. Insert the cardboard in pillowcase.

2. Have an adult help pour dye onto plate. Dip star stamp into dye and press on paper towel to test it. Stamp the pillowcase with rows of stars. Let dry. Use a white marker to outline stars. Use green marker to write Sweet Dreams along the open edge of the pillowcase.

WHAT YOU NEED

For the bugs pillowcase

Washed cotton pillowcase in a light color; iron

Cardboard cut to the size of the pillowcase; pencil

4 or 5 different bug shape crafts foam stamps

Fabric dyes in purple, pink, blue, green, red, and
  yellow; paintbrush; black fabric paint marker

Two 20-inch long pieces of wide ribbon; scissors

HERE'S HOW

1. Ask an adult to iron the pillowcase. Insert cardboard in pillowcase.

2. Leaving about 8 inches of the open end of pillowcase free of designs, use a pencil to lightly draw your face on the pillowcase. Thin a small amount of red dye with water to make soft pink and

paint cheeks. Paint in hair color and earrings if you wish, as shown in Photo A, above. Let dry.

3 Paint the bug stamps, blending colors if you wish, as shown in Photo B. Stamp bugs on the pillowcase around the face, as shown in shown in Photo C. Let dry. Use a black marker to

trace the pencil lines and to detail the bugs. Let dry.

4 Notch each end of the ribbons as shown in Photo D. Put a pillow in the case. Tie each corner of the open end with a ribbon bow.

CONTINUED ON PAGE 78

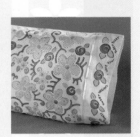

MAYBE I'LL USE PAINT MARKERS TO DRAW MY FRIEND'S FACE ON MY PILLOWCASE!

WHAT YOU NEED

For the floral pillowcase

Washed cotton pillowcase in a light color

Iron; cardboard cut to the size of the pillowcase

Three crafts foam floral stamps

Paintbrush

Fabric dyes in yellow, red, and green

Fabric paint markers in hot pink and black

HERE'S HOW

1. Ask an adult to iron the pillowcase. Insert cardboard in pillowcase.

2. Examine crafts foam stamps to decide if they need more than one color dye on each stamp. If they do, paint the dyes on the stamp with a paintbrush. Stamp designs on the pillowcase until filled with the three floral designs. Let the dye dry.

3. Use a hot pink marker to draw in squiggles to fill in the open spaces, as shown in Photo A, opposite. Let dry.

4. Use a black marker to outline hot pink doodles and add details around flowers, as shown in Photo B. Use black to write words on the open end of the pillowcase. Let dry.

A B

DON'T PUT FABRIC DYE IN YOUR BROTHER'S HAIR OR YOU MIGHT GET GROUNDED!

Buh-bye!

INDEX

Boxes..36–40
Buttons, how to sew 51
CD cases..70–73
Chairs...20–24

DECOUPAGE PROJECTS
   Boxes 36–40
   Chairs 20–24
Frames..16–19
Initials 54–57
Lamps 64–69
Lizzie pictures......................................41–44
Lockers 10–15

PAINT PROJECTS
   Boxes 36–40
   CD cases...70–73
   Chairs 20–24
   Lamps 64–69
   Phones 30–34
   Pillowcases.......................................74–79
   Pillows..26–29

PATTERNS
   Butterfly 52
   Circle 53
   Flower 53
   Heart 52
   Leaf 53
   Lip 29
   Paisley 29
Phones 30–34
Photos, how to use................................45

Pillowcases 74–79
Pillows..26–29
Scrapbooks...58–63

SEWING PROJECT
   Throws...46–53

STICKER PROJECTS
   Boxes 36–40
   CD cases...70–73
   Initials 54–57
   Lamps 64–69
   Lockers 10–15
Stickers ....back of book
Throws..46–53

HMMM... SHOULD I SHARE THESE COOL IDEAS OR KEEP THEM ALL TO MYSELF?!

© Disney 2004.